One blustery day Winnie the Pooh decides to visit his friends in the Hundred Acre Wood. But when he reaches Piglet's fine house in the beech tree, something quite unexpected happens to both of them.

British Library Cataloguing in Publication Data

Disney, Walt
   Walt Disney's Winnie the Pooh and the blustery day.—
   (Ladybird Disney series. no. 845; 3)
   I. Title   II. Milne, A. A. House at Pooh Corner
   813'.54[J]   PZ7
   ISBN 0-7214-0873-7

First edition

WALT DISNEY'S

Winnie the Pooh
and the Blustery Day

Ladybird Books Loughborough

It was one of those blustery days in the Hundred Acre Wood and Winnie the Pooh was sitting in his Thoughtful Spot. This was his special place for sitting and thinking.

Pooh was wondering what to do when he suddenly thought, "Why, it's Windsday! This is my favourite day for visiting friends. I think I'll start with Piglet."

Now Piglet lived in a very fine
house in a large beech tree. When
Pooh arrived, Piglet was sweeping
leaves away from the front door.
"I don't mind the leaves that are
leaving, it's the leaves that are
coming that bother me," said
Piglet.

"Happy Windsday, Piglet!" said
Pooh, but Piglet didn't have time
to say anything back to Pooh...

7

Just then, a gust of wind blew very hard and lifted Piglet into the air.

"Help me, Pooh!" he cried.

Pooh made a grab but only caught the end of Piglet's scarf and the scarf began to unravel like a ball of string.

There was Piglet, flying like a kite, with Pooh holding on to one end of the scarf and running as fast as he could go. Piglet flew over fields and hedges. They went right through Eeyore's house and Rabbit's carrot patch.

KERITS

"Happy Windsday, Eeyore! Happy
Windsday, Rabbit!" shouted Pooh.
Then an even bigger gust of wind
lifted Pooh right off the ground.

The wind blew so hard that Pooh
and Piglet landed high up in a tree
top. And there they were at Owl's
house.

Owl saw them at the window,
waving. He couldn't believe his eyes.

13

Very few of Owl's friends could climb so high in the tree, so it was a special treat for him to have visitors.

"Well!" said Owl. "This is a nice surprise! Do come in for a cup of tea."

He opened the window and Pooh and Piglet flew in.

"Happy Windsday, Owl!" said Pooh.

The wind was shaking Owl's house
backwards and forwards. Then it
blew very hard and the house,
with Owl, Pooh and Piglet
inside, crashed to the ground.

All of their friends from the
Hundred Acre Wood came running
to help.

"I don't think that we will ever be able to fix it," said Christopher Robin, shaking his head. Eeyore was shaking his head too.

"You'll be needing another house, Owl," he said. "It might take a day or two, but I'll find one for you." Everyone thought that this was a very good idea.

The very blustery day turned into a
very blustery night. Outside Pooh's
house it rained and rained. By
morning, the water was very deep
and the Hundred Acre Wood was
flooded.

When Pooh woke up, all the honey pots were floating on the water. Pooh thought that he would eat some honey before it all floated away.

He was licking out the bottom of a honey pot when the water floated him right out of the door.

At Piglet's house the water was
coming in through the window. He
had just written a note which read,
"HELP, PIGLET, ME."

Piglet put the note in a bottle which
floated out of the window and out
of sight. And then Piglet floated
out of the window and out of sight.

Christopher Robin lived on a hill
where the water could not reach.
So everyone made their way to his
house.

Rabbit, Kanga and Roo arrived in a bath tub. Tigger was helping to paddle. Owl was keeping watch from a tree. But there was not a sign of Pooh and Piglet.

It was Roo who spotted the floating
bottle with Piglet's note inside.
Christopher Robin read out the note
and Owl flew off into the wood to
search for Piglet.

As he flew over the flood, Owl saw
Pooh and Piglet floating in the
water. They were not far from
Christopher Robin's hill.

Everyone was waiting at the edge
of the water as Pooh and Piglet
floated in.

"Well done, Pooh!" said
Christopher Robin. "You've saved
Piglet's life. You are a hero!"

"I am?" said Pooh.

Christopher Robin said that as
soon as the flood was over, he
would give a hero's party for
Pooh.

Finally, the rain stopped and Christopher Robin gave the hero's party. Everyone was there except Eeyore. He arrived late.

"I've found a house for Owl," he said. "Follow me."

So they all followed Eeyore through
the Hundred Acre Wood. He led
them right to Piglet's fine house in
the beech tree.

Eeyore stood in front of Piglet's
door and asked everyone to take a
good look at Owl's fine new home.
But everyone looked at Piglet.

"Well…" said Christopher Robin, "this is just the house for Owl. What do you think, Piglet?"

And then Piglet did a Noble thing.

"Yes," he said, "this is just the house for Owl and I hope he will be very happy in it."

Pooh looked at his little friend
and whispered in Piglet's ear,
"That *was* a Noble thing you did."

Then Pooh said loudly, "Piglet,
you can come and live with me."

So Christopher Robin gave a party for two heroes. Pooh was a hero for saving Piglet's life and Piglet was a hero for giving Owl a fine house.

Everyone had a lovely party
and the blustery day turned out
to be not so bad after all.